Discovering
JOBS

Jobs If You Like
SOCIAL MEDIA

Carla Mooney

ReferencePoint
Press®

San Diego, CA

© 2022 ReferencePoint Press, Inc.
Printed in the United States

For more information, contact:
ReferencePoint Press, Inc.
PO Box 27779
San Diego, CA 92198
www.ReferencePointPress.com

LIBRARY OF CONGRESS CATALOGING-IN-PUBLICATION DATA

Names: Mooney, Carla, 1970- author.
Title: Jobs if you like social media / by Carla Mooney.
Description: San Diego, CA : ReferencePoint Press, Inc., 2022. | Series: Discovering jobs | Includes bibliographical references and index.
Identifiers: LCCN 2021030390 (print) | LCCN 2021030391 (ebook) | ISBN 9781678202286 (library binding) | ISBN 9781678202293 (ebook)
Subjects: LCSH: Social media--Vocational guidance--Juvenile literature.
Classification: LCC HM742 .M6577 2021 (print) | LCC HM742 (ebook) | DDC 302.23/1023--dc23
LC record available at https://lccn.loc.gov/2021030390
LC ebook record available at https://lccn.loc.gov/2021030391

CONTENTS

INTRODUCTION: THE GROWING IMPORTANCE OF SOCIAL MEDIA

The COVID-19 pandemic significantly disrupted lives, jobs, businesses, and just about every other aspect of daily life. Many in-person companies and offices closed, while operations and jobs that could be moved online did so. The short-term consequences were severe. Millions of people lost jobs or were laid off temporarily. Others were forced to adjust to working at home.

Connecting Online

The pandemic disrupted in-person interactions and proved how critical it was for businesses to connect with customers via online platforms. April Edwards and her mother, Joy Edwards, are among the many business owners who discovered the power of social media. Their gift store, the Grapevine Cottage in Ontario, Canada, was forced to close multiple times during the pandemic. They had been active on social media beforehand, but faced with catastrophic losses when the physical store closed, they quickly expanded their social media presence. They started actively selling merchandise online through their Facebook business account and other social media profiles. Customers could see all of the store's gift items online and choose delivery or curbside pickup for their purchases. The efforts made by April and Joy to drive sales by increasing their social media activity and engagement ultimately helped their business survive the pandemic. "We had customers drive from two hours away to pick up a special item they saw in a video we posted . . . while the store was temporarily closed. That would have never happened if we had not been active in our social media sharing. . . . It is our digital doorway to the store,"[1] says April.

Their increased use of social media also created a new marketing avenue that the Edwardses plan to continue in the future. April says:

> Social media is what the Sears Catalog used to be. Everyone is using social media and their phones as their shopping guide no matter their age. The Covid-19 pandemic has only made that more evident whether your business is based online, or you have a retail location. I started using . . . social media more when I realized that nobody was going to come walking through the door and I better find ways of sharing my merchandise with customers. I've been pleasantly surprised by the engagement we've received, and what a difference it has made for our bottom line during this rollercoaster.[2]

The Edwardses found that increasing their use of Facebook was the major driver for increasing e-commerce sales. Now they plan to explore new ways to improve the digital and social presence of their business.

The Edwardses are in good company. A survey of chief marketing officers published in February 2021 found that social media was critical to marketing during the pandemic—and continues to be an essential business tool. Companies reported that social media's contribution to overall company performance rose sharply, up 17.7 percent since February 2020. In addition, social media marketing budgets are projected to grow significantly over the next five years, from 14.9 percent in February 2021 to 24.5 percent in 2026. "As the pandemic continues to reshape our world, brands must rethink how they're leveraging social [media] to authentically engage with audiences and deliver unforgettable experiences,"[3] says Jamie Gilpin, chief marketing officer of Sprout Social, a leading provider of social media analytics, engagement, and advocacy solutions for business.

Increasing Opportunities

This is good news for people who want to carve out careers in social media. Prior to the pandemic, career opportunities in social media were already growing. The pandemic emphasized the importance of having employees with the social media skills to handle virtual and social communications through these channels. According to LinkedIn, in January 2021 hiring for digital marketing roles grew nearly 33 percent from the previous year. Experts believe the increased number of social media jobs is not a temporary reaction to the pandemic but is a permanent change. "I see a huge positive shift towards the digital world post-COVID," says Esa Mbouw, deputy head of the Business Administration Program at Swiss German University. "People of all backgrounds are adapting to the digital lifestyle and I predict they will be craving for more social media content. This means social media content would be made and delivered to a wider range of audience in all places."[4]

Social media has changed the way businesses market products and services to customers. "Social media is no longer just another marketing channel or part of a bigger brand campaign. It is *the* connection point between a brand and its audiences,"[5] says Gilpin. This increased reliance on online platforms will continue to create new job opportunities for people who like social media.

SOCIAL MEDIA MANAGER

What Does a Social Media Manager Do?

In most organizations, a social media manager monitors the organization's social media presence, executes its social media strategies, and measures their impact. To do this, social media managers create messaging and content to share across several platforms. This content can be intended to promote an organization's brand, share company information, or publicize marketing campaigns.

Social media managers monitor social media analytics, which is the process of gathering and analyzing data from social media networks. They can use this information when making decisions about what content to create, marketing campaigns, and more. By analyzing the demographics of their reach on social media, social media managers can determine which platform, timing, and format are most effective for their company. For example, a family restaurant might analyze its social media user data and discover that middle-aged women who are married and have children are most active on Facebook from 10:00 a.m. to noon on weekdays. Because the restaurant wants to target this group, it can choose to run its ads during that time frame. This allows the restaurant to reach a greater proportion of its target customers.

Social media managers also spend much of their time creating new content for their organizations. The content

---

A Few Facts

Typical Earnings
Average annual salary of
$53,707

Educational Requirements
Bachelor's degree

Personal Qualities
Strong communication, writing, and time-management skills; creative

Work Settings
Office based or home based

may take the form of pictures on Instagram, short videos on Facebook, blog posts, tweets, LinkedIn articles, and more. These use text, video, and images to build an organization's reputation and help the organization connect and communicate with the public. "I make sure all of our social [media] platforms are telling stories about our museum that people can relate to," says Lanae Spruce, manager of social media and digital engagement at the Smithsonian Institution's National Museum of African American History and Culture. "You never know what to expect, especially when dealing with online content. A fun hashtag might pop up and, if appropriate, we find ways to respond and share our content."[6]

Social media managers measure how well the content performs and how much engagement it drives with customers. They may also be responsible for responding to questions and comments on the organization's social media accounts.

Social media managers often work as part of an organization's marketing department. They may report to a social media director or the leader of content or brand. They often work with

Voice of the Brand

"As a social media manager, you are the front line to every customer, every news outlet, and anyone who comes in contact with the brand. That means you have to be highly aware of everything you say and how you say it. You have to double check spelling, grammar, and tone when posting and you can't let anything slip. One mistake can make or break a post. Everyone is always watching what you do and how you work so be extra careful!"

—Briana Luca, social media manager

Briana Luca, "The Truth About Being a Social Media Manager," Career Queen, 2018. www.careerqueen.com.

other people in the marketing, public relations, and legal departments to coordinate larger marketing campaigns.

A Typical Workday

Social media runs twenty-four hours a day, seven days a week. Most social media managers will start their day by checking on their company's social channels. If there are any questions or comments that need a response, they can take care of them right away. Kristen Griffie is a senior social media specialist for AAA Northeast. At the beginning of each day, she logs in to all of the company's social channels on Instagram, Facebook, LinkedIn, Twitter, and more to check on the overnight activity. "I make sure all content was published seamlessly overnight and that there aren't any outstanding member care requests/comments," she says. "It gives me peace of mind that I can start the day without any immediate issues to address."[7]

Next, social media managers scan news sites for breaking news stories or trending topics related to their organization and their industry. With this information, they can design engaging social posts and content. Creating content is often one of the most important parts of a social media manager's job because it reaches the community and potential customers. "Everyone is on social [media] these days, so lots of people think they know exactly what makes for a good post," says Jake Banas, social media manager at Futurism, a media company focused on science and technology news. "But the role is much more complicated."[8]

After posts are created, social media managers analyze performance. In some larger companies, a social media analyst may perform this role. In order to understand how these campaigns are working, social media managers use a variety of analytics tools. These tools measure engagement on the company's social channels, such as likes, shares, and clicks. Engagement usually leads to website traffic, which can affect company revenue. With all of this data, social media managers evaluate the effectiveness of social campaigns and determine which strategies are most effective at reaching the company's target customers and driving revenue. Griffie says that she reviews analytics reports daily to assess how well content and posts are performing. She uses the information gained from analytics to develop more effective and targeted content for her company's social media channels.

On a typical day, social media managers will also spend time on planning future content for current social media campaigns, as well as developing new strategies to try on various platforms. Often, this planning occurs in meetings. Each week, Griffie holds team meetings to go over upcoming content, content calendars, and strategy. "I also have creative meetings with graphic designers on upcoming needs, as well as get-togethers on special projects and customer service on social [media]. Then there are department-wide check-ins (monthly) and meetings on editorial and paid social [media]. Social [media] marketers usually tend to interact with every department within an organization."[9] Griffie says that one of the most important parts of her job is making sure the organization is publishing quality content on its social media channels. In meetings she makes sure that the company's social media messages are consistent across all channels and incorporate new products and important company news.

Education and Training

Most social media manager positions require a bachelor's degree or higher in marketing, public relations, communications, journalism, or a related field. Many employers prefer to hire candidates who have previous work experience in social media and marketing. They may look for a candidate who has demonstrated success in running social media campaigns or has experience handling social media accounts with a certain number of followers. Candidates should also have a good understanding of social media marketing strategies, along with extensive knowledge of social media channels and reporting tools.

People interested in working as social media managers may choose to earn a certificate in digital and internet marketing. These

Social media managers gather and analyze data from social media networks. They use this information when making decisions about what content to create, marketing campaigns, and more.

programs include training in social media networking strategies, interactive marketing techniques, and social media analytics. Additional certifications such as Google Analytics and Google AdWords are also preferred. Even after they land a job, social media managers must keep up-to-date on new social media trends and platforms, as well as company and industry news.

Skills and Personality

In addition to having extensive knowledge of social media and marketing, social media managers should have strong communication and writing skills. The best social media managers are able to use text, images, and video to enhance their brand's voice on social channels. They know how to write content that connects with their target audience as well as how to make the best use of emojis, GIFs, and pictures to get their message across clearly.

Learning from Mistakes

"When working in a hurry, I have published content with typos. Whenever that happens, I try to recover quickly (editing the posts if possible or deleting them if not), learn from my mistakes, and improve. The nature of the job requires moving at lightning speed, but skipping the fundamentals—such as proofreading and reading for sensitivity—is never worth the cost."

—Mary Kearl, digital and social media marketing leader

Mary Kearl, "The Pros and Cons of Becoming a Social Media Manager," Noodle, October 17, 2019. www.noodle.com.

Social media managers must also be able to communicate well with coworkers and supervisors. They need to be able to clearly explain social media strategy, content plans, and analyses of results. The ability to explain the impact of social media on the business is an important skill for all social media professionals.

In addition, creativity is essential to designing and developing innovative and appealing campaigns that stand out on social media channels. Jim Belosic is the chief executive officer of Short-Stack, a self-service platform used to build engaging campaigns for social, web, and mobile channels. He says:

> To stand out in the crowd, you need to have the ability to create a powerful visual brand across all your social [media] channels, and you need to have a posting strategy that includes a variety of creative and eclectic content, including images, videos, ebooks, promotions, and landing pages. The more diverse your content portfolio is, the better chance you have of being a successful social media manager.[10]

Because they must juggle many tasks, social channels, and campaigns at the same time, social media managers must also be efficient and organized. They need to manage their time wisely, manage content calendars, and execute projects from start to finish.

Because they often interact with customers online, social media managers must be resourceful and have strong interpersonal skills. They listen to customer concerns and demands and need to find ways to resolve them. Understanding customer care allows social media managers to make a positive impression on a brand's followers.

Working Conditions

Social media managers often work in teams, but sometimes they work alone. Frequently, they work in office environments. With internet connectivity, social media managers can often work remotely, checking in with teammates online. Larger companies generally prefer social media managers to work in the office to meet with professionals in marketing and advertising when needed.

Employers and Earnings

Social media managers can work for a wide variety of companies and industries. Some are employed by marketing agencies and provide social media services for clients. According to the job website Glassdoor, as of June 2021 the average salary for social media managers in US companies was $53,707.

Future Outlook

Job opportunities for marketing managers are projected to grow 7 percent through 2029, according to the Bureau of Labor Statistics. This rate is faster than the projected average rate of growth for all occupations. Marketing managers will be in demand since organizations need their skills to maintain and increase their market share. As social media and internet-based strategies become more important to a company's overall marketing strategy, candidates who have social media and digital marketing skills and experience should have the best opportunities.

Find Out More

American Marketing Association

www.ama.org

The American Marketing Association is a professional association for marketing professionals. Its website has information about marketing careers, certifications, industry news, and various publications.

Digital Marketing Association

www.dmaglobal.com

The Digital Marketing Association is a professional association for digital marketing professionals. Its website has information about digital marketing careers, education resources, a blog, digital marketing resources, and other useful links.

Digital Marketing Institute

https://digitalmarketinginstitute.com

The Digital Marketing Institute is a company that provides information and training for digital marketing careers. Its blog has many articles about careers in digital and social media marketing. Other resources include podcasts, videos, micro lessons, and more.

Social Media Association

www.socialmediaassoc.com

The Social Media Association was formed as a place where professionals can learn, share, and empower business through social, digital, and future media. Its website features a blog, articles and news about social media, member spotlights, and information about upcoming events.

CONTENT STRATEGIST

What Does a Content Strategist Do?

Digital and social media marketing relies on great content. Digital content can include blog posts, podcasts, videos, photos, and more. This content appears on company websites, email blasts, and social media channels. Content marketing focuses on creating and distributing valuable content to attract and retain a target audience. The ultimate goal of content marketing is to increase brand awareness and profits.

Who develops great content for a company's digital channels? That is the job of a content strategist. Bradley James Morin, the head of content and growth at 12up, a global sports media and technology company, explains that a content strategist's job is to "create content that resonates with [an] existing fan base, yet is differentiated and engaging enough to draw in new, underserved or overlooked consumers."[11]

Content strategists plan, develop, and produce content to be used on all of a company's digital platforms. They plan, write, and edit content. Sometimes they manage a team of content creators and writers. Overall, content strategists make sure that all content is clear, compelling, and consistent with an organization's brand and philosophy. "As a content strategist, I use data, research and my understanding of psychology to shape my client's narrative and create content experiences tailored to the company's

A Few Facts

Typical Earnings
Average annual salary of $100,661

Educational Requirements
Bachelor's degree

Personal Qualities
Strong writing and storytelling skills, attention to detail, communication and organizational skills

Work Settings
Office based or home based

target audience,"[12] says Chantel McGee, a content strategist who works with several tech start-up companies. Once the content is created and approved, content strategists make sure that it is distributed across an organization's web, mobile, and social media channels.

Content strategists may also be responsible for creating and maintaining an editorial calendar that details what content will be published, as well as where and when it will be published. In some companies, content strategists create style guides for content creators to ensure that all content across the company has a similar style and feel even when created by different people. In larger companies, the content strategist may manage other employees and freelancers who create content for social media, web, and mobile channels.

A Typical Workday

A content strategist often spends time planning and creating social media campaigns and other digital content on a typical workday. Part of their research involves search engine optimization (SEO) keywords. SEO is the practice of increasing the amount and quality of traffic to a website through search engine results. Content strategists research to find the best keywords to use in content to drive traffic to the site. Once they have a list of keywords, they will write compelling content using those keywords that will be published on the company's website, social media platforms, and other digital sites. If working on a multimedia project, a content strategist may spend some time on video production, audio production, or photography.

After posting content, a content strategist will regularly check to see how it is performing. Is the content driving engagement on social media channels? How is it performing on search engines? How is it impacting website traffic? The content strategist will use this data to analyze how content performs and how to improve it in the future. Says Jacquelyn Jacobsma, a creative content strategist for a digital marketing agency, "For a creative content strate-

Measuring Content Success

"While it's difficult to measure content success or understand a competitive landscape without access to proprietary analytics, publicly available search and social [media] data can give us clues as to what's working and what's not in a particular niche. That means no day goes by without time spent manipulating massive Excel spreadsheets. As a result, my desk mates always know who to ask when they need help with pivot tables and macros. I usually start with SEO by investigating what keywords a client currently ranks for organically. Then I suggest alternative keywords they should prioritize in future content."

—Kristen Poli, manager of content strategy services at Contently, a company that helps clients create great content

Kristen Poli, "A Day in the Life of a Content Strategist," Contently, September 18, 2017. https://contently.com.

gist, simply producing work isn't our only job. During and after a particular client campaign, we analyze results. What worked, and what can we improve? Through Google Analytics and other tools, we analyze our work, then take what we've learned and adapt it to the next project."[13]

Georgie Cauthery is a content strategist at Raconteur Media Company, a digital marketing company. In her role, she develops content for a variety of clients and projects. Her client services team produces content such as research reports, online articles, infographics, and videos. She and her team also advise clients on content strategies and messaging. Cauthery says:

A typical day for me might be meeting with a client to come up with an idea for a campaign, briefing one of our fantastic designers on a new project, writing a creative brief for a journalist, editing some copy or creating a narrative for an infographic and finding data to tell the story. A lot of my projects also involve coming up with concepts for proprietary research, designing the surveys and then analyzing the data to pick out the most interesting trends to create a piece of content about.[14]

Being able to satisfy a client is one of the job's highlights for Cauthery. "I get massive job satisfaction from knowing our clients love and get value from what we create for them, so it gives me a real boost every time I get an email telling me how beautiful their content looks or how they've used it to reach their goals,"[15] she says.

Education and Training

Most content strategist positions require a bachelor's degree or higher in English, journalism, communications, marketing, technical writing, or a related field. Many employers prefer to hire candidates who have several years of work experience as a digital content manager, web writer, or content editor.

Possessing writing skills and being able to tell a story are essential to the job. "I firmly believe the best content strategists have a background in journalism and a fundamental understanding of how to tell compelling stories," says McGee. But "it's not enough to be a good writer; you should also be able to produce video and understand how to tailor that content to different digital and social media platforms,"[16] she adds. McGee believes that having multimedia, multiplatform experience is more important than having a specific type of educational degree. She suggests that students look for an internship that provides hands-on experience in copywriting, analytics, and multimedia tools.

People interested in a career in content strategy should also have training and experience with SEO techniques and content management systems. They should also know how to use social media management tools such as Hootsuite and Buffer. A working knowledge of programming languages such as HTML, CSS, and JavaScript is also beneficial.

Research skills are another vital part of content strategy. Content strategists often need to learn about a complex topic and create related content that readers can easily understand. Matthew Speiser, who leads content strategy at the content intelligence platform Knotch, says:

> In order to do that, you need to have a strong grasp of the topic yourself. This requires research. I personally read at least 5–10 articles on a subject I'm writing about before I even put pen to paper. I also make it a best practice to reach out to experts on the topic in order to get unique insights—an old habit I picked up as a journalist. Research also helps you develop your expertise in the industry you work in, which will help you be seen as a thought leader.[17]

Skills and Personality

In addition to solid writing and storytelling skills, excellent communication and planning skills are essential for this career. Content strategists often work closely with social media strategists, designers, and marketing and sales professionals to design and implement a unified marketing strategy.

Content strategists focus on the big picture when creating a company's content strategy. Yet they must also be able to pay attention to the tiniest details. They must understand the importance of every word to improve search engine performance. They must be precise when editing content for every word, image, video, and more.

Analytical skills are also crucial in the job. Content strategists monitor and analyze how content performs and use that information to improve future content. Often, they work on multiple projects for multiple clients simultaneously. Therefore, strong organizational skills are essential to make sure they keep all projects on schedule without sacrificing quality. "As I'm usually working with multiple clients at once, time management is a necessary skill to be effective. I've learned to react quickly under pressure and prioritize tasks accordingly, something that has aided tremendously in my success,"[18] says Jamie Maddison, a senior content strategist at NewsCred, a content marketing services company.

Generating Ideas

"One of the biggest parts of my role is to come up with ideas for campaigns. After some initial research on the client and their industry, I'll get a feel for the type of content that resonates well and start brainstorming ideas that would be worthy of links. I will then organize an ideation meeting with the rest of the team where we'll all bring our research and thoughts and decide on a campaign that we all agree will work best."

—Chris Tucker, senior content strategist

Quoted in Chloie Brandrick, "A Day in the Life of Chris Tucker, Senior Content Strategist," Click Consult, February 4, 2019. www.click.co.uk.

Working Conditions

Content strategists typically work during regular business hours; however, freelance strategists may have more flexibility. Content strategists often work in teams with others but can work alone at times. Frequently, they work in office environments. With internet connectivity, content strategists can often work remotely, checking in with teammates online. "Whether you work well from nine to five at the 9 Clouds headquarters, at a coffee shop over the lunch hour, or on your couch at home at midnight—just work where and when you work your best. It's as simple as that,"[19] says Jacquelyn Jacobsma.

Employers and Earnings

Content strategists can work for a wide variety of companies and industries. Some work for a digital, publishing, or media company, where they create content for clients. According to the job website Glassdoor, as of June 2021 average salary for content strategists in the United States was $100,661.

Future Outlook

As more companies shift to targeted marketing using digital channels, the demand for talented people who can develop and manage content will remain strong. "Content marketing continues to gain traction as a lead generation tool amongst companies of all sizes," says Diane Domeyer, executive director of the Creative Group, a marketing and creative staffing company. "Agencies and in-house teams seek experienced content strategists who can create, curate, and syndicate content to increase brand awareness and conversation rates."[20]

Find Out More

American Marketing Association

www.ama.org

The American Marketing Association is a professional association for marketing professionals. Its website has information about marketing careers, certifications, industry news, and various publications.

Content Marketing Association

https://the-cma.com

The Content Marketing Association is an industry association for marketing, publishing, advertising, and social media professionals. Its website features podcasts, case studies, news, and webinars about content marketing.

Digital Marketing Association

www.dmaglobal.com

The Digital Marketing Association is a professional association for digital marketing professionals. Its website has information about digital marketing careers, education resources, a blog, digital marketing resources, and other useful links.

Digital Marketing Institute

https://digitalmarketinginstitute.com

The Digital Marketing Institute is a company that provides information and training for digital marketing careers. Its blog has many articles about careers in digital and social media marketing. Other resources include podcasts, videos, micro lessons, and more.

COMMUNITY MANAGER

What Does a Community Manager Do?

With millions of daily active users, social media companies offer a variety of platforms that can be used by businesses to increase awareness and build a brand. Companies like Netflix and Taco Bell have become well known for their witty tweets and personable interactions with their followers on social media.

Social media is also where a brand can show its personality. Brand personality is more than the voice and tone of a tweet or post. It reflects what a brand stands for and connects a company's product to its consumers. According to a 2017 Sprout Social survey, nearly 75 percent of consumers value humor in a brand's personality. They also appreciate honesty, helpfulness, and friendliness on social media. How does a company build a reputation on social media that incorporates all of these qualities and remains true to the company's unique voice? That is the job of the community manager.

Community managers are a liaison between an organization and its audience on social media. They are the voice, tone, and moderator of the brand. They build and maintain a brand's community—its followers—both online and offline. They are also responsible for managing the public's perception of a brand or company. To do this, community managers engage with audiences in a variety of ways

A Few Facts

Typical Earnings
Average annual salary of
$55,489

Educational Requirements
Bachelor's degree

Personal Qualities
Strong interpersonal, communication, organizational, and time-management skills

Work Settings
Office based or home based

and places. They interact with audiences in an online forum or on a social media network. They reach out to audiences at in-person groups or other places. No matter where they interact with consumers, community managers must be the brand's consistent tone, voice, and personality. Ultimately, their efforts to engage their audience can increase awareness of their brand, improve public perception, and improve the company's performance.

How a community manager engages with audiences can differ significantly by the organization. For example, a community manager for a local gym might develop challenges to encourage member participation and have members post progress on social media. The community manager might also manage a Facebook group or other social community for members, in which he or she offers training tips and health information for a specific audience. All of these actions engage members and build the gym's community both online and offline.

Because community managers directly interact with an organization's followers, they are the first to see the audience's response to new content and marketing programs. Often, they record and report these responses to the company's content strategists and marketing professionals. This information from community managers can help a company tweak a marketing or content strategy to more effectively engage with the target audience.

A Typical Workday

On a typical day, a community manager starts his or her day by checking all of the company's social media channels and pages. If there are any unanswered comments or new inbox messages, the community manager responds. Once that is done, the manager might scroll through social media, websites, and other portals for any relevant news or information that would interest the community. The manager plans new content for the upcoming day and future content for the week and month. He or she checks in on current social media campaigns to see how they are performing and whether they are hitting the intended target market.

The manager creates new content and posts it to the pages and sites he or she manages. And throughout the day, the manager constantly checks his or her social media sites, looking for new engagement from followers and responding to any comments or questions.

Kirby Reynolds is a community manager at Birchbox, a beauty subscription box service. Every day, she responds to customer comments and questions across the company's social media accounts, including Facebook, Instagram, Twitter, and YouTube. With more than 2.4 million followers, that can add up to a lot of activity every day. Lately, Snapchat has become Reynolds's favorite social platform on which to interact with customers. "I respond to everyone who's written in and give a bunch of product recommendations. I love doing Snapchat since the customer can quickly, easily and privately show concerns, the service is very personal. I could chat there with our followers all day," she says. She has also started engaging with customers on Facebook Live. "We record a Facebook Live video, and I sit in to respond in real-time as people ask questions during the stream," she says. "We've recently started doing these live feeds and they've been really successful. Like Snapchat, these streams feel very personal and are a great opportunity for customers to ask questions and for us to kind of have a conversation with them."[21]

In the course of her day, Reynolds sometimes has to deal with an angry customer. However, she does not let it bother her. "I can't ask a customer to not be passionate about what we do," she says. "Negativity on our channels doesn't bring me down—for me, it's a chance to reassure the customer."[22]

Education and Training

Community managers can have a variety of backgrounds. However, most have experience with communications, public relations, and social media. Most community manager positions require a bachelor's degree or higher in journalism, marketing, English, public relations, or a related field.

Using Customer Feedback

"We think about story ideas and posts that will be relevant to our box theme and explain products we will sample. I contribute feedback from customers that I've seen on social [media] and as a group we discuss incorporating this feedback into our April plans. In addition to the insights I give in this type of meeting, I send a weekly report to team leads with feedback from customers on social media so everyone, including people whose roles don't have them interacting with customers, knows what our customer thinks and feels."

—Kirby Reynolds, community manager at Birchbox

Quoted in Hilary Milnes, "Day in the Life: How Birchbox's Community Manager Responds to 200 Customers a Day," Digiday, February 23, 2016. https://digiday.com.

Many employers prefer candidates who have job experience with marketing, sales, or social media. They also look for candidates who can demonstrate strong writing skills. To get some experience in these skills, candidates can maintain active social media accounts, blog, or do freelance writing. Those interested in this career can also gain valuable experience by volunteering to work on marketing campaigns and community building for nonprofit organizations.

Once hired, community managers work closely with a company's marketing and sales departments. New hires may train with professionals in those departments to learn more about the company and its marketing and sales activities.

Skills and Personality

For any community manager position, superior communication skills are essential. Community managers must have strong written and verbal communication skills to form connections with consumers on various social media and digital platforms.

Community managers juggle multiple responsibilities at once across several platforms. They interact with customers online and in person, create new content, respond to comments and questions, and more. Organizational skills are essential to keeping content and communications up-to-date across all outlets.

Time management is another critical skill in this career. Community managers must be able to set and keep deadlines for social media campaigns and special events. Their audiences expect prompt responses, and community managers must dedicate a portion of every day to daily interactions no matter what other projects arise.

Working Conditions

Community managers usually work full time in an office environment. Most of the time, their work is performed at a computer. They meet regularly with team members, clients, and other company professionals.

Community managers are a liaison between an organization and its social media audience. Through interaction with consumers, they become the voice, tone, and moderator of the organization's brand.

Sometimes, community managers may work remotely. Monina Wagner is a social media community manager for the Content Marketing Institute (CMI). She works remotely. She says:

> The CMI team uses Skype for Business. This gives us the ability to instant message and place video calls. Even when we're not under the same roof, we can see each other! When I first started with CMI, I hated telecommuting. It was not what I envisioned. I missed cubicle life. But once I set up my office and learned how to use Skype for Business, I realized I was much more productive working from home (or even working from Starbucks) than I ever was in an office.[23]

Sometimes the job requires working nights and weekends. "Social media is a 24/7 job, and yes, I am held accountable by our community and our thousands of followers," says Wagner. "There will inevitably be times when I must work on a weekend or in the middle of the night because of a social media crisis. It's part of the job. But spending time away from the computer reinvigorates me; 'real life' inspires my 'social' life."[24]

Employers and Earnings
Community managers can work for a wide variety of companies and industries. Some work for a digital, publishing, or media company, where they create content for clients. According to the job website Glassdoor, as of June 2021 average salary for a community manager in the United States was $55,489.

Future Outlook
According to the Bureau of Labor Statistics, job opportunities for public relations specialists, which includes community managers, are projected to grow 7 percent through 2029. This rate is faster than the projected average rate of growth for all occupations. Organizations will continue to need public relations specialists to maintain and enhance their reputation and visibility in the market.

The Future of Community Management

"Community managers will have to be more creative in how they approach, engage, and nurture communities. Many brands will soon take online relationships offline. They will reward members for their support and feedback by hosting in-person events. They will want to know members more intimately through local meetups. Online forums and social media can be the catalyst that starts relationships but a community manager can take it to the next level by fostering that relationship in unexpected ways offline."

—Monina Wagner, social media community manager at CMI

Dennis Shiao, "A Day in the Life: Content Marketing Institute's Community Manager," Medium, April 26, 2017. https://dshiao.medium.com.

The increased use of social media is expected to create more opportunities for public relations specialists who work in these platforms, including community managers.

Find Out More

American Marketing Association

www.ama.org

The American Marketing Association is a professional association for marketing professionals. Its website has information about marketing careers, certifications, industry news, and various publications.

Content Marketing Association

https://the-cma.com

The Content Marketing Association is an industry association for marketing, publishing, advertising, and social professionals. Its website features podcasts, case studies, news, and webinars about content marketing.

Digital Marketing Association

www.dmaglobal.com

The Digital Marketing Association is a professional association for digital marketing professionals. Its website has information about digital marketing careers, education resources, a blog, digital marketing resources, and other useful links.

Social Media Association

www.socialmediaassoc.com

The Social Media Association was formed as a place where professionals can learn, share, and empower business through social, digital, and future media. Its website features a blog with articles and news about social media, member spotlights, and information about upcoming events.

MARKETING MANAGER

What Does a Marketing Manager Do?

Customer engagement is at the center of any successful business. Marketing allows businesses to develop and maintain relationships with their customers. Marketing managers actively plan, direct, and coordinate a company's marketing policies and programs. They work closely with a company's sales, public relations, and product development teams.

Marketing managers research the demand for a company's products and services and the demand for the products and services offered by its competitors. They research and identify potential target markets for the company's products and services. They are involved in new product development and research market trends to identify customer needs that new products or services can fill.

Marketing managers develop pricing strategies for the company's products and services. They aim to price products and services at a level that maximizes profits or market share while also satisfying customers.

In today's digital world, a large part of a marketing manager's job involves managing a company's social media and other digital platforms. Marketing managers ensure all social media platforms and campaigns follow company guidelines and standards. Marketing managers also develop marketing campaigns, including digital campaigns, from idea to final analysis.

A Few Facts

Typical Earnings
Average annual salary of $142,170

Educational Requirements
Bachelor's degree

Personal Qualities
Creativity, leadership, strong communication and organizational skills

Work Settings
Office environment

They may plan promotional campaigns such as contests or give-aways.

Daryn Edison is a marketing manager at RSAWEB, an internet service provider in South Africa. He describes his job:

> As a marketing manager, I am responsible for the marketing budget, strategy, planning and execution—ensuring all is done in line with the objectives of the business. I drive brand growth and customer experiences by putting people first and using data to improve strategic decisions. I'm accountable for all marketing activity of the brand and the success of the company. A large part of my job is also to build each team member, helping to achieve their own personal and career goals. Operationally, I make sure the department runs smoothly, that all projects and tasks are done on time and with no errors.[25]

A Typical Workday

Lynnsay is a marketing manager who works within the agency team at Raconteur Media, a digital marketing company. "I work closely with the account directors on my team to design campaigns that will engage our target audience and generate leads, as well as help them with proposals and pitches that they are preparing for potential clients," she explains. Lynnsay spends her day managing the marketing plan for Raconteur Media and also working on projects for Raconteur clients when her marketing strategy and digital marketing skills are needed. "This means that my 'day-to-day' is difficult to describe—I can be planning our events strategy, setting up digital ad campaigns, attending client meetings, writing copy and so much more on any given day. It means I'm kept very busy—but it's amazing to work across such a diverse range of tasks. Every day is different!,"[26] she says.

For Edison, a typical day begins by holding a daily meeting with his team to review the projects and tasks everyone is working

Predicting Trends

"Analyzing and predicting trends—for everything from product launches to social media. Even though this is one of my favorite things [to] do when I get it right, planning content and marketing campaigns can sometimes feel like a shot in the dark or playing the lottery. Especially with crazy news dropping multiple times a day, our collective attention span is constantly changing."

—Annie Rogerson, senior marketing manager at Artisan Talent

Quoted in Artisan Talent, "A Day in the Life of a Marketing Manager," February 2, 2021. https://creative.artisantalent.com.

on that week. After the meeting, he reviews any creative work that needs his approval to move forward. Then he may have additional meetings with staff, clients, other departments, and vendors. Over lunch he reads the latest industry news and researches market trends. Then he spends the rest of the day reviewing analytics on current projects and campaigns, planning new campaigns, and providing feedback on creative work. "I enjoy the diverse nature of the job," he says. "Marketing is no longer just about advertising and sales, it involves all aspects of the business including support, development, IT infrastructure, finance, operations, etc. I get to work with many different stakeholders and have contact with a number of different people at all levels."[27]

Clair O'Neill is a marketing manager for a boutique hotels website, i-escape. In her role, she is responsible for driving traffic to the company's website. "This involves managing our search marketing strategy, developing exciting brand partnerships, working with agencies to run display retargeting campaigns and analyzing the digital data we gather from our acquisition channels," she says. She also spends time building relationships with similar brands and influencers to help grow awareness of i-escape. A typical day starts with a review of a revenue report for the previous day.

Then O'Neill opens Google Analytics to see daily traffic statistics and check in on how all of the company's current marketing campaigns are performing. She says:

> Today I finished writing a blog on a recent visit to Sri Lanka (I know, super lucky). I rarely get time to write in this role so it's a real treat for me now. I then checked our web project management tool to see if there were any technical tickets that needed a response from me. . . . This afternoon I'll be getting my head into an email campaign and creating dashboards for Google and Bing paid ads as we're going to manage these in-house soon.[28]

Education and Training

Most marketing managers have a bachelor's degree in marketing, communications, computers and information technology, or a related field. Some employers prefer candidates with a master's degree in a related field. Students interested in a career as a marketing manager can take classes in marketing, consumer behavior, market research, sales, communication methods, and visual arts.

In addition, many employers prefer to hire candidates with previous experience in the field. According to CareerBuilder, nearly 50 percent of marketing managers have at least ten years of experience in the field. Many marketing managers have work experience in advertising, marketing, promotions, or sales. To gain experience, candidates first work in lower-level marketing positions such as a marketing coordinator or a specialist role.

Skills and Personality

Marketing managers must have a blend of traditional marketing and digital skills. Written and verbal communication skills are essential because marketing managers must communicate effectively with managers, staff, vendors, and customers. This includes giving presentations to company and client management. Creativity is also vital since marketing managers often develop new and creative marketing ideas and campaigns. Because their role requires them to interact with many different people and personalities, interpersonal skills are also crucial for success in this role.

Strong leadership, organizational, and time-management skills are important since marketing managers guide a team of marketing professionals. They juggle multiple responsibilities at once across several projects and campaigns. They must be able to set and keep deadlines for marketing campaigns and events. Being organized can help them successfully plan and execute long-term marketing strategies.

Today's marketing managers need to have digital skills as well. "Technology is unleashing new levels of creativity for marketers and enabling connections with people that we couldn't have even imagined years ago," says Marc Pritchard, global marketing and brand-building officer at Procter & Gamble. "Young marketers today have a huge advantage because they are avid users of the emerging technologies."[29] Marketing managers should understand search engine optimizations and be able to optimize a company's web presence on search engines. They should be familiar with Google Analytics and other web analytics reporting. Marketing managers often oversee a company's social media channels. Therefore, managers should stay up-to-date on the latest social media platforms and trends. They should also be familiar with paid search platforms like Google AdWords and Bing Ads to promote their company digitally. Identifying ways to optimize a company's website can also improve revenue and increase customer satisfaction.

Working Conditions

Marketing managers usually work full time in an office environment. They meet regularly with team members, clients, and other company professionals. Some marketing managers travel to different locations from time to time. For example, a marketing manager in the retail industry may have to visit retail stores to make

Incorporating Partnership Stories

"We love to elevate and amplify partnership stories in as many ways as possible, so this work can also take on different forms. I may meet with an influencer marketing leader from our customer TechStyle to prep her for a fireside chat recording. . . . Or I'll chat with an influencer network about their best practices for forging and optimizing new partnerships with brands. . . . These brand and partner stories don't just turn into case studies, video testimonials, and blogs—they also contribute to our voice-of-customer validation and guide us to make more informed product, packaging, and positioning decisions."

—Molly Doyle Young, product marketing manager for the internet marketing and technology company Impact

Quoted in Talking Influence, "A Day in the Life: Molly Doyle Young, Product Marketing Manager at Impact," June 16, 2020. https://talkinginfluence.com.

sure employees are trained on a new promotion. When a deadline approaches, marketing managers may need to work late or over the weekend to ensure the project's deadline is met.

Employers and Earnings

Marketing managers can work for a wide variety of companies and industries. Some of the largest employers include professional, scientific, and technical services companies (23 percent); management companies (14 percent); finance and insurance (10 percent); manufacturing (9 percent); and wholesale trade (8 percent). According to the Bureau of Labor Statistics' *Occupational Outlook Handbook*, the median annual wage for marketing managers was $142,170 as of May 2020.

Future Outlook

According to the Bureau of Labor Statistics, job opportunities for marketing managers are projected to grow 7 percent through

2029. This rate is faster than the projected average rate of growth for all occupations. Marketing managers will be in demand since organizations need their skills in order to maintain and increase their market share. As social media and internet-based strategies become more important to a company's overall marketing strategy, candidates with social media and digital marketing skills and experience should have the best opportunities.

Find Out More

American Marketing Association
www.ama.org
The American Marketing Association is a professional association for marketing professionals. Its website has information about marketing careers, certifications, industry news, and various publications.

Digital Marketing Association
www.dmaglobal.com
The Digital Marketing Association is a professional association for digital marketing professionals. Its website has information about digital marketing careers, education resources, a blog, digital marketing resources, and other useful links.

Digital Marketing Institute
https://digitalmarketinginstitute.com
The Digital Marketing Institute is a company that provides information and training for digital marketing careers. Its blog has many articles about careers in digital and social media marketing. Other resources include podcasts, videos, micro lessons, and more.

Internet Marketing Association
www.imanetwork.org
The Internet Marketing Association is a professional organization for people in digital marketing, sales, design, and more. Its website features links to news stories, industry news, press releases, and newsletters focused on digital and internet marketing.

SOCIAL MEDIA INFLUENCER

What Does a Social Media Influencer Do?

Not long ago, businesses did not have as many choices for getting the word out about their products and brands. Some paid for product promotions by popular actors, athletes, and other celebrities. Such people were paid to wear a brand's clothing and use their products in public. Mass media coverage of the celebrities would put the brand's products in the spotlight, too.

With the rise of social media, this type of marketing is no longer limited to well-known personalities. Today almost anyone who has a large following on social media can become a social media influencer. Social media influencers gain followers by creating and sharing quality content. They inspire, entertain, inform, and connect with followers. They interact with followers, start conversations on social media, and drive engagement.

Social media influencers often have a specific niche—such as fashion, beauty, lifestyle, food, toys, technology, or travel. They have built a reputation on their knowledge and expertise in their particular niche. They make regular posts on social media about their topic. Their dedicated followers see them as experts in their niche and pay close attention to their views and recommendations. As a result, social media influencers are well positioned to set trends and work with brands to encourage their followers to buy the brand's products and services.

A Few Facts

Typical Earnings
Varies

Educational Requirements
None

Personal Qualities
Authenticity, interpersonal and communication skills, multitasker

Work Settings
Varied, home-based office

Social media influencers may have a large following across several social media platforms or specialize on one platform. Each platform gives influencers a different way to create, publish, and consume content and engage with followers. For example, Instagram influencers create highly visual content and assign each photo or video a short text caption. In contrast, YouTube influencers create longer video content. Other common social media platforms for social media influencers include Facebook, Twitter, TikTok, and Snapchat.

A Typical Workday

Style influencer Courtney Seamon is one of two creators of *Mimosas and Manhattan*, a blog that features fashion, interior design, beauty, and travel content. When Seamon and her cousin Kelly McFarland started the blog in 2013, it was simply meant to be a creative outlet and a hobby. Since then, running the blog and its associated Instagram account has turned into Seamon's full-time job.

On one typical day, Seamon attended a breakfast with other social media influencers at a trendy restaurant in SoHo, a neighborhood in New York City. Bed Bath and Beyond hosted the breakfast to promote its sleep products. Seamon and the other attendees received a sleep mask and were given a form to order a complete set of sheets and blankets. The company hoped the social media influencers would post favorable comments on their social media accounts about the products.

Seamon says that she gets invited to many similar events around New York City. She evaluates how each could positively impact her business before deciding which events to attend. She attends events to make connections or to build partnerships for the future. "You have to think of everything as a business move," Seamon says. "You have to ask yourself, 'Is it going to pay off in the long run?'"[30]

After the breakfast, Seamon headed to a pop-up shoe store for a one-on-one consultation with an online shoe designer. She

Don't Give Up

"This field becomes more and more saturated every day, and these social media platforms' algorithms seem to change every hour. Tenacity is what will keep you pushing through the frustrations, failures, and setbacks. Tenacity will make putting in the ungodly hours feel like an investment in something bigger instead of a hole that you're digging yourself into. You can be unique, talented, beautiful, and well-educated, but without tenacity, you will never survive the ebb and flow that is social media influencing!"

—Gabby Beckford, twenty-four-year-old travel influencer

Quoted in ShareThis, "20 Social Media Experts Reveal the Most Important Traits for a Successful Social Media Influencer," January 14, 2020. https://sharethis.com.

snapped photos of the shoes and her other activities during the day. Before posting the photos to her Instagram Stories, Seamon carefully edited each one with an app on her phone.

Next, Seamon headed to a local park, where she met a friend who snapped photos of her and her outfit from different angles and backgrounds. Once she had enough photos, Seamon returned to her apartment, which doubles as her office. At home, Seamon posted blog content. She also posted sponsored photos from brands that are paying her to help promote their products on her Instagram account. To keep the Instagram account feeling authentic to her followers, Seamon tries to keep the account 80 percent content from her day-to-day life and 20 percent sponsored posts from brands that pay her.

Next, Seamon selected outfits for an upcoming video on the blog that will show followers how to transition from fall outfits to warmer winter clothing. She estimates that the one-minute video will take a few hours to create, with setup, makeup, multiple takes, and editing. Seamon says that most people who see in-

Social media influencers gain followers by creating and sharing quality content. They inspire, entertain, inform, and connect with followers often in a particular niche, such as fashion, beauty, lifestyle, food, toys, technology, or travel.

fluencer photos do not realize all the work behind the scenes. "Nobody gets what we do," Seamon says. "They just see the pictures. But people don't know all the work that went into it."[31] Then she changed into her second outfit of the day and headed out for two additional events and more photos.

Education and Training

There is no specific education or training required to become a social media influencer. What a person does need is a knowledge of social media, the ability to create appealing and engaging content, and a substantial number of followers. "There is no guidebook to do what we're doing," says Seamon. "There's no major on how to do it. We had to figure it out as we go."[32]

Most social media influencers start by establishing their specialty or niche. They choose a niche based on their personal interests. Once they have identified their niche, people who want to become influencers should choose which social media platform to focus on. Do they prefer photos or video? Does their content shine with longer blog posts? Also, where is the target audience? For example, an influencer targeting businesspeople might find LinkedIn a better social platform than TikTok for their content.

Then social media influencers develop a content strategy. What do they plan to post, and how often? What type of content will generate the most engagement as measured by likes, comments, shares, and clicks? Once the content is posted, influencers need to create engagement with their followers and develop a relationship. By monitoring analytics and metrics, social media influencers can measure whether their efforts are succeeding.

Skills and Personality

One of the essential traits of a successful social media influencer is authenticity. "People follow real, genuine people who know their stuff. They don't want flaky wannabes who are clearly just in it for attention and the money. . . . Those characteristic traits go a long way to building your following and reach which is then key for being a true [social media] influencer,"[33] says Alistair Dodds, marketing director and cofounder of EIC Marketing, a digital marketing agency in London.

Interpersonal and communication skills are also essential. Social media influencers do more than just post interesting content online. They engage with and develop a relationship with their followers, making the followers more likely to trust their recommendations on brands. "I believe that the most important skill for a successful social media influencer is the ability to create and connect with his/her network and create a sincere relationship with the followers. I've seen many social media people fail to create a following solely because they didn't have this required drive to connect with people and bring people to them,"[34] says Jakub Kliszczak, a marketing specialist at CrazyCall, a calling center software company.

Influencers who hope to establish themselves on social media need to post content often and on a consistent schedule. This takes discipline and organizational skills. Networking is another valuable skill. Social media influencers spend a good deal of time with other influencers and brands at industry events. Networking to build relationships can help them land new paid partnerships and gain followers.

Working Conditions

Most social media influencers work for themselves. As a result, they often use their home as an office base. They spend a lot of time attending influencer and industry events to network with other social media influencers and brands. Depending on their niche, they visit brands and other places to create content. Travel influencers spend a lot of time traveling to gather material and create content for their social platforms. Because social media is a 24/7 communication tool, influencers often work many hours to attend events and engage with followers, even at night and on weekends.

Employers and Earnings

Most social media influencers work for themselves and make money through several avenues. Those with enough followers can charge companies a fee per post for a sponsored post or become a brand ambassador, which is a person paid to represent a brand in a positive light. In the beginning, companies might offer to pay the social media influencer in free products. However, as an influencer's followers grow, he or she can negotiate fees with the brand.

Some social media influencers join an influencer network. The network provides connections to brands that are looking for social media influencers. It also provides a community of support for influencers, especially for those just starting their careers.

Once social media influencers have gained a big enough following, they can make money selling products for their own brand or area of expertise. For example, the fashion and lifestyle blog *Living in Yellow* sells custom T-shirts and sweatshirts. Some prominent influencers even get paid to make appearances at events, launch parties, and more.

A social media influencer's earnings can vary from a few free products to hundreds of thousands of dollars. According to a 2021 report from CNBC, an Instagram influencer with a minimum of 5,000 followers and 308 sponsored posts a year can earn up to $100,000.

Future Outlook

Today it is easy to find social media influencers all over the internet. With each post, influencers increase brand awareness and have a significant impact on a company's image. As a result, influencer marketing is currently one of the biggest marketing trends. Brands are increasingly turning to less-well-known influencers to feature their products. As the popularity of unfiltered and less scripted content increases, the everyday social media influencer will be more in demand.

Find Out More

American Influencer Council (AIC)

www.americaninfluencercouncil.com

The AIC is a trade association for influencers and content creators. Its website has a resource hub with business development tools, links to industry news, and information about programs for members.

American Marketing Association

www.ama.org

The American Marketing Association is a professional association for marketing professionals. Its website has information about marketing careers, certifications, industry news, and various publications.

Digital Marketing Institute

https://digitalmarketinginstitute.com

The Digital Marketing Institute is a company that provides information and training for digital marketing careers. Its blog has many articles about careers in digital and social media marketing. Other resources include podcasts, videos, micro lessons, and more.

Influencer Marketing Association

www.influencermarketingassociation.org

The Influencer Marketing Association was established in 2018 as the first official trade organization committed to defining, growing, and protecting influencer marketing. Its website has information about joining the organization.

SOCIAL MEDIA ANALYST

What Does a Social Media Analyst Do?

For a person who loves social media and working with data and numbers, a job as a social media analyst may be a perfect fit. Every day, customers scroll, click, and engage on social media. All of this activity creates an enormous amount of data for companies to use. However, this data is only helpful if a company can gather and analyze it to create meaningful information that drives a company's decision-making. That is why more companies are turning to social media analysts to help them make sense of their social data.

Using various analytics tools, social media analysts note recurring patterns, evaluate content types that consistently drive engagement, and track the way different content types perform over social channels over time. They track the effectiveness of social media marketing campaigns. With this information, companies can create more targeted content and apply these insights to larger marketing campaigns. In some cases, social media analysts might even gather product feedback.

For example, a company's content creator may want to understand which types of artwork perform the best on social networks. A social media analyst can gather data that shows customer engagement with the different types of artwork. This information helps the content creator decide which artwork to use. Then the analyst can monitor engagement data

---

A Few Facts

Typical Earnings
Average annual salary of $49,356

Educational Requirements
Bachelor's degree

Personal Qualities
Analytical skills, communication skills, digital and computer skills

Work Settings
Office environment

Sharing Insights

"If a brand is seeing a significant boost in engagement on a specific type of content, sharing this insight with content producers and community managers will help us to tweak our content mix accordingly. If a particular strategy or program is struggling and generating lower than expected results, sharing this insight with strategists and client teams provides opportunities to brainstorm new tactics and solutions. If we see significant negative sentiment through social monitoring about a particular product or brand, alerting the account lead can provide a quick alert to the client and kickstart crisis communication."

—Jessica Hammerstein, social media analyst

Jessica Hammerstein, "A Day in the Life of a Social Media Analyst," Ignite Social Media. www.ignitesocialmedia.com.

to see whether there needs to be any adjustments to the recommendation.

Analysts do more than present data. They also analyze it to understand why specific trends are happening. For example, if engagement on a social channel is down from one month to the next, analysts investigate the decline to understand why it happened. They use analytics tools, study historical performance data, and look for any specific circumstances impacting the drop in engagement. They might dig into comments and negative messages to see whether any information might explain why the content is underperforming.

Analysts look beyond a specific company's data to study industry and competitor data. Doing so allows them to understand better what strategies work in the industry, where there are gaps in a company's content, and ideas to help a company stand out from competitors. Analysts also use social monitoring and social listening tools to find out what people are saying online about their brand, competitors, and the industry. With this information, analysts can identify what matters to consumers and how best to engage with them on social media.

A Typical Workday

Jessica Hammerstein is a social media analyst at Ignite Social Media, a social media marketing company. She works with a variety of clients to analyze their social media performance. On a typical day, Hammerstein spends a lot of her time collecting, aggregating, and analyzing social media usage and engagement data from many different sources. She uses analytics tools such as Facebook Insights, Twitter Analytics, YouTube Analytics, and Google Analytics. She also uses paid media reporting tools, such as Facebook Ads Manager and Twitter Ads, and other social analytics tools to pull all of the relevant data related to channel and content performance.

Once she has the data, Hammerstein searches for trends, interesting stories, insights, and abnormalities to help clients understand what is happening on social media. "Analyzing social data provides a great opportunity to prove the worth of social strategy, showcase where a brand can grow and improve," she says. Hammerstein also creates easy-to-understand reports for clients and company personnel. "Because staring at an Excel spreadsheet full of numbers can be confusing and anxiety-inducing for many right-brained individuals, reporting is also an essential role of an analyst," she says. "We need to be able to identify key insights and information, visualize the data, and provide context in a way that is digestible and easy to understand."[35]

Hammerstein collaborates with many different people in her job, including community managers, content producers, account leads, strategists, and more. One of the most important parts of her job is ensuring that the correct information is given to the right person. She loves the job's combination of social media and numbers, she says:

> From the outside, a social [media] analyst's job can look like endless numbers and Excel spreadsheets. However, for a data nerd like me, being able to dig in and uncover trends, abnormalities, and opportunities in social [media] data and transform those findings into actionable insights for internal teams and clients makes the job interesting and challenging. I get to crunch data for clients across a variety of industries, and get an understanding for how different strategies perform.[36]

Education and Training

Most social media analysts have a bachelor's degree in marketing, communications, public relations, or a related field. Analysts should also be good with numbers. They may have a background or degree in statistics, data science, computer programming, or a related area. Since the job involves working with large amounts of data, being able to manipulate spreadsheets and databases is an important skill to have.

Social media analysts should also have a strong understanding of how different social networks operate. Hands-on experience with social media platforms and digital marketing campaigns is also beneficial. Some employers prefer candidates who have previous work experience in social media.

Analysts also should have a good understanding of search engine optimization for online content, keyword research, and social media analytics tools. Experience working with social media monitoring tools such as Google or Twitter Search and social media management tools such as TweetDeck and Hootsuite are a plus. Some positions also require analysts to use analytics tools such as Google Analytics and other internal reporting tools.

Using Data to Create a Customer Profile

"Customer profiling is a way of understanding your customers in more detail by identifying characteristics that are unique to distinct customer groups. This is achieved by drawing data from a variety of demographics and dimensions, such as age, gender, interests and hobbies. Personas are created from the findings to help put a face to the customer data. Knowing to whom you're marketing means that you can tailor your messaging and tactics appropriately to increase conversion and secure a positive return-on-investment."

—Adam Read, senior data analyst

Adam Read, "Answering Difficult Questions: A Day in the Life of a Data Analyst," Further, September 6, 2017. www.further.co.uk.

Skills and Personality

In addition to technical and marketing skills, social media analysts must have strong analytical skills to interpret social media data and provide valuable information for clients and company personnel. They also need to connect what they are seeing in the data to what it means for human behavior. Reinhardt Schuhmann, a product manager at TRACX, a company that provides a cloud-based social media monitoring system, says:

> In many cases the numbers can point to several characteristics of a customer group that is active in social [media], but qualitative research is required to tie these together and produce a fully fleshed out customer profile. . . The best social media analysts I know are the ones that can take data-based findings and translate them into insight about the actions, thought, and feelings of people. The data might show thirty emergent trends from people talking about

basketball, but a good social analyst will be able to determine that eight of those trends represent the behavior of a single audience segment.[37]

In addition, strong written and verbal communication skills are essential in this role because analysts must communicate and clearly present their analysis and ideas to coworkers and clients. Social media analysts juggle multiple responsibilities at once across several platforms. Multitasking and organizational skills are essential to keeping up with all their responsibilities across various platforms. Time management is another important skill in this career, since analysts must be able to meet deadlines.

Working Conditions

Social media analysts frequently work in office environments. With internet connectivity, social media analysts can often work remotely, checking in with teammates online. Often, social media analysts are part of a larger team that includes marketing, public relations, sales, and product development. Because social media is online twenty-four hours a day, seven days a week, analysts may be asked to work outside of regular business hours.

Employers and Earnings

Social media analysts can work for a wide variety of companies and industries. Some are employed by marketing agencies and provide social media services for clients. According to the job website Glassdoor, as of June 2021 social media analysts in the United States earned an average salary of $49,356.

Future Outlook

According to the Bureau of Labor Statistics, job opportunities for market research analysts, which includes social media analysts, are projected to grow 18 percent through 2029. This rate is faster than the projected average rate of growth for all occupations.

Market research analysts will be in demand as businesses continue to develop and increase their social media presence and strategies. This means that job opportunities for people with social media and digital marketing skills will continue to grow.

Find Out More

American Marketing Association
www.ama.org
The American Marketing Association is a professional association for marketing professionals. Its website has information about marketing careers, certifications, industry news, and various publications.

Digital Marketing Association
www.dmaglobal.com
The Digital Marketing Association is a professional association for digital marketing professionals. Its website has information about digital marketing careers, education resources, a blog, digital marketing resources, and other useful links.

Digital Marketing Institute
https://digitalmarketinginstitute.com
The Digital Marketing Institute is a company that provides information and training for digital marketing careers. Its blog has many articles about careers in digital and social media marketing. Other resources include podcasts, videos, micro lessons, and more.

Social Media Association
www.socialmediaassoc.com
The Social Media Association was formed as a place where professionals can learn, share, and empower business through social, digital, and future media. Its website features a blog with articles and news about social media, member spotlights, and information about upcoming events.

SOURCE NOTES

Introduction: The Growing Importance of Social Media

1. Quoted in GlobeNewswire, "Ripl Helps Small Businesses Increase Sales Through Social Media During Pandemic," April 19, 2021. www.globenewswire.com.
2. Quoted in GlobeNewswire, "Ripl Helps Small Businesses Increase Sales Through Social Media During Pandemic."
3. Quoted in Gary Drenik, "The Next Generation of CMOs Will Come from Today's Social Media Managers," *Forbes*, September 29, 2020. www.forbes.com.
4. Quoted in Emma Wiltshire, "Social Media Marketing Post-COVID: Marketers Predict the Future," Social Media Today, July 16, 2020. www.socialmediatoday.com.
5. Quoted in Drenik, "The Next Generation of CMOs Will Come from Today's Social Media Managers."

Social Media Manager

6. Quoted in Notre Dame of Maryland University, "Career Path: Social Media Manager," September 21, 2017. https://online.ndm.edu.
7. Quoted in Sophie Maerowitz, "Sneak Peek: A Day in the Life of a Social Media Manager," PR News, 2021. www.prnewsonline.com.
8. Quoted in Greta Rainbow, "'Social Media Manager' Is One of the Most Popular Jobs in the US. It's a Lot Harder than It Sounds," Money, June 26, 2020. https://money.com.
9. Quoted in Maerowitz, "Sneak Peek."
10. Jim Belosic, "5 Skills to Master Before You Even Think About Applying for a Social Media Job," The Muse, 2021. www.themuse.com.

Content Strategist

11. Quoted in Jenell Talley, "What Does a Content Strategist Do?," Mediabistro, 2021. www.mediabistro.com.
12. Quoted in Talley, "What Does a Content Strategist Do?"
13. Jacquelyn Jacobsma, "A Day in the Life of a Creative Content Strategist at 9 Clouds," 9 Clouds, September 19, 2017. https://9clouds.com.
14. Georgie Cauthery, "A Day in the Life of a . . . Content Strategist," Raconteur Media, March 5, 2020. https://careers.ra conteur.net.
15. Cauthery, "A Day in the Life of a . . . Content Strategist."
16. Quoted in Talley, "What Does a Content Strategist Do?"
17. Matthew Speiser, "What Does a Marketing Content Career Path Look Like?," Knotch, August 3, 2020. https://prosand content.knotch.com.
18. Quoted in Ben Davis, "A Day in the Life of . . . a Content Strategist," Econsultancy, October 23, 2017. https://econsul tancy.com.
19. Jacobsma, "A Day in the Life of a Creative Content Strategist at 9 Clouds."
20. Quoted in Robert Half, "Hot Job: Content Strategist," *The Robert Half Blog*, February 6, 2019. www.roberthalf.com.

Community Manager

21. Quoted in Hilary Milnes, "Day in the Life: How Birchbox's Community Manager Responds to 200 Customers a Day," Digiday, February 23, 2016. https://digiday.com.
22. Quoted in Milnes, "Day in the Life: How Birchbox's Community Manager Responds to 200 Customers a Day."
23. Quoted in Dennis Shiao, "A Day in the Life: Content Marketing Institute's Community Manager," Medium, April 26, 2017. https://dshiao.medium.com.
24. Quoted in Shiao, "A Day in the Life."

Marketing Manager

25. Quoted in RSAWEB, "A Day in the Life of a Marketing Manager," February 11, 2020. www.rsaweb.co.za.

26. Lynnsay, "A Day in the Life of a . . . Marketing Manager," Raconteur Media, March 10, 2020. https://careers.raconteur.net.
27. Quoted in RSAWEB, "A Day in the Life of a Marketing Manager."
28. Quoted in Ben Davis, "A Day in the Life of a Marketing Manager for a Boutique Hotels Website," Econsultancy, April 18, 2017. https://econsultancy.com.
29. Quoted in *U.S. News & World Report*, "Marketing Manager," 2021. https://money.usnews.com.

Social Media Influencer

30. Quoted in Paige Leskin, "I Spent a Day Following an Instagram Influencer Around New York City to See What Her Job Was Really like—and It Was Way More Work than I Expected," Business Insider, January 2, 2020. www.businessinsider.com.
31. Quoted in Leskin, "I Spent a Day Following an Instagram Influencer Around New York City to See What Her Job Was Really like—and It Was Way More Work than I Expected."
32. Quoted in Leskin, "I Spent a Day Following an Instagram Influencer Around New York City to See What Her Job Was Really like—and It Was Way More Work than I Expected."
33. Quoted in ShareThis, "20 Social Media Experts Reveal the Most Important Traits for a Successful Social Media Influencer," January 14, 2020. https://sharethis.com.
34. Quoted in ShareThis, "20 Social Media Experts Reveal the Most Important Traits for a Successful Social Media Influencer."

Social Media Analyst

35. Jessica Hammerstein, "A Day in the Life of a Social Media Analyst," Ignite Social Media. www.ignitesocialmedia.com.
36. Hammerstein, "A Day in the Life of a Social Media Analyst."
37. Reinhardt Schuhmann, "What It Takes to Be a Social Media Analyst," Social Media Today, October 3, 2015. www.socialmediatoday.com.

INTERVIEW WITH A SOCIAL MEDIA MANAGER

Sarah Hurley is a social media and digital marketing manager at the University of Pittsburgh's Clinical and Translational Science Institute in Pittsburgh, Pennsylvania. She has worked in digital marketing for twelve years and social media marketing for nine years. She answered questions about her career by email.

Q: Why did you become a social media manager?

A: It was kind of an accident. I had a communications and English degree. I got a job as an editorial assistant at a media company after graduation. I learned about writing for an online audience, search engine optimization (SEO) and community management. I was laid off in 2008 when the market fell out. I applied for everything I could. I was hired as a digital marketing assistant at a family-owned trophy and awards company. They taught me a lot about digital marketing and what they couldn't teach me, I learned by taking training classes at Google's offices in [New York City] and following who I could online (people and brands). I loved learning about it. It felt a little bit like psychology. I had to think about what people would search for, what imagery would catch their eye, what wording would resonate with them. It was fascinating. My next position brought social media into my world and it felt like a nice marriage of my editorial experience and my digital advertising knowledge. It was early in social media and it was a different world than it is today.

Q: Can you describe your typical workday?

A: No, haha! It's always a bit different. I try to break my day into a few different areas. First thing is checking any notifications that came in overnight and reviewing any scheduled posts for the day.

I do this before I even dive into my email. Email can often come with lots of requests for posts. A lot of the job is educating folks in the organization that don't know the strategy behind social media marketing. My week is filled with different meetings with all areas of the organization to talk about their projects and how social [media] may be able to help. For larger organizational campaigns, I work with marketing teams on how paid efforts will fit in with a larger advertising effort. I have a monthly content calendar of broad topics that I review each week when I finalize the posts and schedule them out. I don't like scheduling out too far, as I need to be flexible for in-the-moment changes/requests as well as national and local news events that could impact scheduled posts . . . I end each day reviewing what I have planned for the next day, posts and meetings.

Social media can be 24/7. There are ways to set expectations with customers/users about when responses can be expected, but there is still a level of after-hours/weekend/holiday effort. If you're a one-person team, you still have to pay attention to anything that comes through. If you're on a larger team, you can create a schedule of who is covering when. That said, if something comes up that requires attention, you may be brought in, whether you're on coverage or not.

Q: What do you like most about your job?
A: It's always changing. Platforms, norms, rules all evolve and change regularly. It keeps me on my toes and forces my knowledge to stay relevant. I do also love sharing that knowledge with people and being an evangelist of sorts around how organizations can use social media and digital marketing efforts for good, in a thoughtful and positive way.

Q: What do you like least about your job?
A: Primarily, that often people feel they can do my job because they have a personal social media presence. Management of a profes-

sional presence is not the same as posting personal pictures and viral memes. So there's a lot of educating folks in the organization, which in many ways I actually love that part of my job, but it can be tiresome having to prove yourself to people in other departments.

Q: What personal qualities do you find most valuable for this type of work?

A: • Creative or analytical (this role can require being both, but I'm not sure one can truly be both). I tend to be more analytical and envy the creatives.

- Flexible, as mentioned above, plans can change very quickly, but you also should be organized and prepared so when there aren't any priorities to push out, you still have content ready to promote.

- Customer-oriented with tough skin. You will be the first responder to complaints and issues. People take their anger with a brand out on social [media]. Know that even though you are reading it, it is not being directed at you. That can be hard. I still feel the sting when I read them. That said, appreciate these people. They care enough to give you feedback to help your organization and an opportunity for service recovery. Don't discount the value of that. It's when people start tuning you out that you've lost them. You will also get the joy of being the first to see amazing messages of praise and joy and the best part is being able to share those stories. Social media is named that for a reason . . . you're being social. Don't make it a one-way conversation.

- Able to communicate effectively. You're going to present information in a variety of ways from 280-character tweets to executive-level presentations throughout your career. Know your audience and communicate with them in a way that they will hear you.

- Storyteller. Know how to tell a good story. That's what you're doing in this field. The content you're pushing out is a story of the brand or organization you represent. Learn how to tell it in a way that people will care about.

57

Q: What advice do you have for students who might be interested in this career?

A: Join associations and groups online to soak up as much as you can; shadow people in different types of roles for different organizations; get certified; once you enter the workforce, focus your search on organizations where you won't be a one-person team, as you'll want to have people around you to learn from and be a gut-check on your decisions.

OTHER JOBS IF YOU LIKE SOCIAL MEDIA

Art director

Blogger

Brand ambassador

Brand manager

Communications specialist

Copywriter

Digital communications
professional

Digital content manager

Digital marketing manager

Digital media manager

Digital media producer

Director of social media

Director, social marketing and
brand communications

Director, social media
marketing

Director, social media relations

Email marketing specialist

Engagement coordinator

Film and video editor

Graphic designer

Interactive media coordinator

Internet marketing
coordinator

Internet marketing manager

Multimedia communications
specialist

Online content coordinator

Public relations specialist

Search engine optimization
specialist

Social media assistant

Social media coordinator

Social media designer

Social media strategist

Editor's note: The online *Occupational Outlook Handbook* of the US Department of Labor's Bureau of Labor Statistics is an excellent source of information on jobs in hundreds of career fields, including many of those listed here. The *Occupational Outlook Handbook* may be accessed online at www.bls.gov/ooh.

INDEX

PICTURE CREDITS

ABOUT THE AUTHOR

Carla Mooney is the author of many books for young adults and children. She lives in Pittsburgh, Pennsylvania, with her husband and three children.